Sigria

FREE TO REJOICE

TRACEY JERALD

Believe in miracles!

xoxo,

Tracey Jerald

FREE TO REJOICE

Free to Rejoice

ISBN: 978-1-7324461-4-4 (eBook)

ISBN: 978-1-7324461-5-1 (Paperback)

Editor: One Love Editing (http://oneloveediting.com)

Editor: Trifecta Editing Services (https://www.trifectaedit.com/)

Cover Design: Amy Queau – QDesign (https://www.qcoverdesign.com)

To my readers. This is my gift for loving the
Freeman's as much as I do.

And to D.B. You taught me some men will get down on their knees holding a
platter of chocolate to make you smile. You were an amazing boss, an
amazing leader, and an inspiration.

Thank you for taking the time to get to know the man in my life because
you just knew he would mean something to me. I only wish you could have
seen me marry him. Thank you for making sure I was told about the
cookies after you were gone.

You will forever be missed.
12/24/2005.

1

"Tell me the truth. You rigged the Secret Santa to draw Keene's name deliberately, didn't you?" I ask my husband.

Phil's innocent look doesn't fool me for a minute. "I'm shocked that you would think I'd rig something as important as Secret Santa, Jace. That would be unethical," he huffs, throwing his nose in the air.

"Changing Ali's work password to 'Phillipa<3u' so she would consider naming their baby after you isn't unethical?" I retort.

"That was merely a minor faux pas, my love. I meant for it to be 'Phillip<3su.' I was so happy to have her back after she was gone." He blinks his long-lashed blue eyes at me so innocently, I'd believe him regardless of what he said or did.

It's not the innocent face or the words that come from his lips. It's his hands. And they're jammed in his pockets, so I can't determine the truth.

Phil and I have been together for ten years, since the summer he and his sisters moved from the South to Collier, Connecticut. He fell into my life when one of his youngest sisters, Corinna, pulled him into Candlewood Lake. Phil's fall into the water was only fair as he was trying to throw Corinna in it at the time.

Years haven't dimmed the love I have for this man. In fact, every day that passes, I wake up even more blessed when I see the perfect ripples of his muscled back lying next to me in bed. And regardless of what ungodly hour I have to wake up to leave to drive to the hospital for my shift, my husband is at the door, sleepily handing me a to-go coffee and a kiss to carry me through the long, and often heartbreaking, hours until I can see him again.

Medicine was my first love, and despite years of sacrifice, exhausting hours, and hospital bureaucratic bullshit, it astounds me every day that I've been blessed with a miracle.

Phil is my miracle. God showed his humor when he crafted the only man I'll ever love. A man with the face of an angel, but a will that would try the Devil himself. He created a man with a sense of honor so profound for those he loves—Phil sacrificed everything for his adopted sisters, but none so much as he did for his oldest sister, Cassidy, who we recently found out is Keene's biological sister.

There's been tension between the two men as they've learned to adapt to the changes in their shared sister's life—including her falling in love, finding out who she really is, her recent marriage, pregnancy, and the birth of her beautiful twins.

Phil supported Cassidy as she blossomed into her womanly strength after her early years stripped it from her. Keene is still struggling with the years he missed since his Cassidy was taken from him when she was four—years he can never recover. And that is why, Keene isn't comfortable with what Phil sacrificed to save his sister, because he feels it should have been him.

Lord knows I wasn't when I first found out, but I soon realized if it wasn't for the gift Phil gave Cassidy, the chain reaction of events that happened never would have occurred: Phil and Cassidy would never have found an unspeaking Emily in a park after her parents were killed. They wouldn't have connected later with Alison, Corinna, and Holly, who were living in a battered women and children's shelter after being rescued from a human trafficker.

He never would have moved to Connecticut with his "family," fallen into a lake, and he never would have met me.

I love this man from the bottom of my soul, but some days, even for me, it's hard to reconcile the Phil who sacrificed so much with the Phil who relentlessly needles Keene about sex. Which brings me back Phil's Christmas gift for Keene. If I volunteer to go pick up Phil's gifts, maybe I can intercede if Santa's most devious elf went too far off his rocker. Traipsing around the mall sounds like punishment to someone like me, who's been done shopping since before Thanksgiving, but I'll do it. Not exactly how I planned my first day off, but why the hell not? If I stick around the house, I'm sure Phil's going to come up with a "honey-do" list full of crap we absolutely don't need done before Christmas morning.

"I'm off until after the holidays, babe." A holiday miracle unto itself. Seven full days starting today where I'm not expected at the hospital. Forget gifts—this is all I need. Taking a sip of coffee from one of the white mugs, I sink into our leather couch. "I can go shopping this afternoon."

Phil scoots closer from his side of the sofa. "Well, since you volunteered..."

"Anything for you." And to save all of us celebrating Christmas. "Just tell me what you need."

A wicked smile crosses Phil's face. My stomach lands somewhere around my bare feet, which are being rubbed. "I'll text you what I need. But later."

Placing his coffee mug on the floor, my husband prowls over my body and engages me in a long kiss that eliminates all thought from my brain except one.

Mine.

By the time Phil tugs my sweater over my head, I'm no longer worried about Christmas. The only thing I give a damn about is feeling the heat of my husband's body sliding over my skin, the way his lips crashing against mine. I quiver when I feel the strength of his lean muscles in my hands. Seeing the surprise in his bright blue eyes when I roll him over to trail my lips down the muscles bisecting his chest is better than any gift that will be opened on Christmas morning.

~

I SWEAR I've been had—and not in the way Phil took me on our couch this morning.

Goddamnit, who in their right mind leaves all of their Christmas shopping until three days before Christmas? With a mental sigh of resignation, I answer myself. My husband. That's who.

The list he handed me, with a lingering kiss, was a page long. Typed. While I gaped at him, he was at least able to tell me everything was ordered and paid for. All I had to do was brave the Danbury Fair Mall to pick everything up.

With that encouraging news, he strode around muttering about making another "damned wreath with holly and bloodying his hands." Since this is the one time of the year where Phil's being a florist actually causes him physical pain, I held him just a little closer before letting him race out the door.

I thought I'd get a jump on the holiday shoppers, but I should have known better. People are insane. Then again, right now, so am I.

I'm following—honestly, stalking—a woman as she pushes a stroller laden with packages to her car. I'm driving myself nuts between the blinker sound as cars whip around me looking for a space and my fervent prayers that this woman doesn't cut between cars to another aisle. All the while, my radio continues to play chirpy Christmas music, which started out cheerfully but now has me wondering if I'll need a dental appointment after the new year from clenching my molars so tightly.

It's two long minutes later when she stops at an SUV. I see my prey open her trunk. Oh, God, it's filled with packages. What if she's not leaving? I begin to panic, sweat dripping down the middle of my back. No... Yes! She's leaving! She quickly unsnaps her baby carrier and plops her child into the car. As a doctor, I approve of her taking care of her baby's needs first.

Then begin her struggles with her packages. Five minutes later, I'm this close to jumping out and helping her load her car when she finally finishes. Deck the halls, baby! I'm in business. I've never seen

Christmas lights as beautiful as the ones reflecting off of her tailgate as she slams it closed.

Out of the corner of my eye, something flashes. My jaw falls open as a black sports car jerks out from behind a long line of cars at the end of the aisle, its engine roaring to life. I shake my head at the idiocy of the driver as the car weaves in and out. The car slows to a purr before picking up speed. I snarl possessively, "Hell no, mother-fucker. That's my parking spot," before my doctor instincts kick in when I quickly realize he's about to crash into the woman. "Shit," I mutter, slamming my car in park and bracing.

The sound of a car crash is disgustingly abhorrent and cruel: the squeal of the tires on the pavement, the initial shatter of the flimsy outer body terrifying as pieces of windshield and fiberglass fly in all directions, some of them striking my car.

I couldn't care less.

I'm out of my car seconds after the impact is over, my lungs seizing as I try to move as fast as they'll go to get closer. Even as I stumble, I witness the car back away from where it trapped the woman against the back of her car, hesitating briefly, before speeding off, narrowly avoiding sideswiping me in its bid for escape.

Though I'm devastated by what I'd just witnessed, I'm grateful I can hear the wretched sound of the woman's breathless agony. It means she has a chance. "Ma'am? Ma'am, what's your name?" I call loudly to be heard over the increasing cacophony of sound as witnesses begin to amass in a protective ring.

"Mary," she says weakly. "Hurts. Hurts so badly."

"I'm Dr. Jason Ross. I'm an ER doctor. I was behind you waiting for your parking spot. I want to check on your baby before I assess your injuries, Mary." My words are as clear and as precise as they can be. "If the baby is safe, do you give me permission to move him to my car?"

"Her," she murmurs weakly. "Her name is Grace. Eight weeks old."

"Okay. Let me get Grace to safety first, then we'll take care of you."

I race around the back of the car, praying I'll find the car seat undisturbed.

When I reach the door, I find an angel. Grace's eyes are welled up with tears, and her rosebud lips are a perfect bow even though they're howling with displeasure. I sigh in relief. Pushing down on the buttons to release the infant car seat, I lift her before spotting her diaper bag. Grabbing both, I hurry to my own vehicle, sliding them inside. I race back to Mary and lean over her. "Grace is safe. Her car seat was installed perfectly. Did you do that?"

Mary shakes her head against the ground. "Her father. He's a fire-fighter."

"He did a good job. You did a good job. She's safe."

"Good." Mary's eyes flutter closed.

"Mary? Mary. I need you to keep talking to me. Help is going to come soon. I can't move you until I get a board. Tell me what you were shopping for today," I demand. Reaching over, I touch one of her hands. Her pulse is thready. I can see the ground around her beginning to tinge with red. She's bleeding from somewhere.

Fuck.

"I was getting Joe—that's my fiancé—some new clothes for a family photo." Her voice is getting weaker. "Just one perfect photo of all of us." Tears well in her eyes. "Why did this happen, Doctor?"

I stroke my hand over her face, trying to brush the debris away. "I wish I knew, Mary. Take comfort in the fact Grace isn't hurt, and that we're going to get you fixed up."

A tear slips down the side of her cheek. "It was going to be our first Christmas together," she gasps, right before her head lolls to the side. She's unconscious, and a trickle of blood is dripping from her mouth.

Fortunately, emergency services arrive and comes over to where I'm waving and yelling madly. "Here! Over here! We have injuries!"

One of the wagon drivers calls to his partner before jogging over. "Get the board!"

When he reaches me, I rattle off everything I know. "Patient is a two-months postpartum Caucasian woman. Her infant is in the front seat of my car." I point to my vehicle and one of the EMS personnel goes sprinting in its direction. "She was putting away her packages when the other vehicle came at her at an undetermined speed, hitting her head-on. She appears to have internal injuries. Her purse is in the back seat." The EMS nods as he takes her blood pressure before calling out, frowning, "BP is low."

He leans over to listen with his stethoscope, something I itch to grab out of his hands. I can have her triaged and ready to go in a matter of seconds—seconds that could determine her life or death on this brittle winter day.

"She's not breathing. Preparing for intubation," he calls out to his partner.

I lean over and begin to run my hands over her body. Is that a distention near her lower abdomen? "What the hell are you doing?" he snaps.

"I'm an ER trauma specialist at NYU." My voice holds every ounce of authority I use when I'm on duty. "Have someone grab my bag from the trunk of my car."

"Shit. We'd be happy to have you along for the ride, Doctor."

My smile is grim. "I wasn't planning on going anywhere."

As he prepares her for blind intubation, I grope for my bag, digging to find my own set of ears. Pressing it against her tummy, still enlarged from her pregnancy, I hear something of concern. And that's nothing at all.

There should be some sound, something to let me know there's blood flowing through her bowels. Hearing nothing is worse than hearing the gurgles.

"Call ahead," I urge the EMS technician. "Make sure there's an ultrasound ready. I think she's bleeding internally from either her uterus or her intestines."

"Load her up! Doc, you're riding with us."

Quickly, I scramble into the back of the ambulance, getting out of the way of the EMTs. Holding Grace on my lap in her car seat, I mentally urge Mary to hold on, to keep fighting.

The heavy doors slam, and soon we're in motion toward Danbury Hospital.

Grace begins to fuss with the wail of the sirens. Even as I root around for her pacifier—which thankfully is clipped to her warm puffy outerwear—I listen for a moan, some indication that Mary's in pain. Instead there's no sound other than the equipment the EMT is using to keep her alive until we reach the hospital.

I slip the pacifier in Grace's mouth, and her little mouth takes root. The soft sucking heightens the desperation in the small space as the fight to keep this mother alive begins.

A shudder runs through me, caused by much more than the winter cold.

TEN HOURS LATER, I stagger into the front door of my home with Phil, utterly drained.

Mary didn't make it. The internal bleeding was too intense.

I was there when they told her fiancé, Joseph Bianco. In hours, he went from being a proud new daddy to a single father of a baby girl. I was there when he broke looking down at his daughter and whispered, "But I don't know what do without her."

And I was there when, as so many grief-stricken people do, he blamed me for not doing things faster.

"How could you be right there and not manage to save her?"

Those words might haunt me for some time. Too often patients come in, and the time between when they wreck or when they make the decision to go to the ER makes it impossible to save them. Today, I was right fucking there, and I still couldn't do it. I couldn't save her.

I couldn't pull off a miracle.

Even as I was assuring the safety of her child, she was slowly bleeding to death.

Intellectually, I know there was nothing I could have done.

But try telling that to my heart.

Leaning against the wall, I slide until my ass is resting on my heels. Burying my face into my hands, I rub hard and fast, trying to scrub away the pain.

"Jace." The most beautiful sound in the world.

My head snaps to the side, and he's there. My redemption. I called him earlier when Mary was in surgery to let him know what had happened. He told me to take care and that he loved me. I know he can see the outcome in my face. We've been together for so long, I don't have to say a word.

This is what finding your soul mate is like.

And my heart breaks all over again, knowing that for Joe and Grace, their souls were permanently shattered.

"Come with me, sweetheart. Let me take care of you."

Pushing myself to my feet, I reach for my husband's hand, letting him shower his endless love on me even as he bathes the aftermath of the day from my skin and my soul.

2

I wake up the next morning feeling less bruised and battered. Judging by the winter sun in the sky, I know I've been left to sleep late. Since I have nowhere to be, I luxuriate in the softness of the sheets I so rarely get to enjoy. I'm shocked when my foot brushes up against something in the bed.

"Jesus, Phil. You're late!" I fling back the covers and swing my legs over the side of the bed before I'm hauled back in, up against my husband.

"Relax, babe. I talked with my sisters last night. I don't need to be in for hours." He strokes my back as our bodies naturally ease together, each groove and hollow finding their perfect resting place. I hear Phil's heart beat against my ear and know in a symphony of sound, there's nothing that compares to that of the one of love.

I know he'll have to spend an ungodly amount of hours racing around trying to finish up everything in time for the holiday now only two days away. But he's here with me after a hellacious day and night. I'm about to speak when I feel long fingers graze along my hip. My cock stirs. "Jesus," I whisper, unable to control my body's response to him after all these years.

Phil's knowing smile comes from years spent learning my body.

His bright blue eyes are filled with budding excitement, but more importantly, they're filled with tenderness. "I keep telling you, my love. I'm not Jesus."

My head rolls back and forth on the pillow as my husband drops his head to nibble on my collarbone, his hands holding me captive simply because they're touching my body. They're rough and tender as they skim over my chest.

Heat pours off Phil's body, drawing me like a warm fire on this cold December morning. I shove away the covers between us and press my body against his, trapping our cocks between us. We both let out a simultaneous groan.

Phil's arms band around me. Our mouths meet in a kiss that obliterates all thought from my brain. This is scorching, incinerating. Yanking back with a snarl, he thrusts his fingers through my hair and pulls it back so he can drag his teeth down my throat. My hands find purchase on his ass. I'm already rocking into him, wanting more. Needing.

It's always need with Phil.

I can't help but need him.

I place kiss after kiss on his warm skin, needing the taste of his cologne mixed with sweat on my tongue—that is, until he pulls away. I let out a hiss of displeasure until I feel my husband's lips brush against my chest, then make their way south over my flat stomach.

My breathing picks up as he spends his time licking and sucking around my hip. I'm surprised my cock isn't stabbing him in the eye as he switches from one side to the other, driving me insane with long licks followed by the scrape of his teeth.

"I need..." That's all I manage to get out before Phil's hand and mouth covers my cock at the same time, and I almost levitate off the bed.

He removes the heat of his mouth to taunt, "You always react like that."

"Less talking and more sucking. God." My head flops back because despite what I said, he isn't wrong. Every time since the first time, and more times than I can count anymore, I do still react like that. Like I'm something to be worshipped, cherished, and sexualized all at the same time.

Need pulsates through me, driving me closer to the edge. My hips thrust up against Phil's face, which he can barely control with one hand shoving them back against the mattress. "I want you to explode in my mouth, Jace. I want to suck you until you're screaming from the pleasure I give you." Feral blue eyes meet my dark ones. "And I know just how to do it."

Over my labored breathing, I hear the quiet snick of the cap.

Yes! I know just where this is going.

My body is desperate in its need to release. I know Phil will shove me over the edge soon. Between his mouth sucking me, his one hand jacking what he can't fit in his mouth, and now his other hand coated in lube circling my rim, I start squirming.

And when his first two fingers thrust into my ass, I'm in a frenzy. My head shoots back, and my eyes close as I groan out my delicious agony.

"Fuck...yes...Phil...right there. God, baby. I'm gonna blow." Without much warning, I'm filling his mouth up as he continues to fuck me with his hand and suck me back down until I'm a quivering mess on our bed.

As I come back down from the high of being taken, I see my husband lazily stroking his cock and balls, looking like a tame lion eyeing his prey. Relaxed, I lean back, my body on full display. "See something you want?" I taunt, shifting my legs open.

Phil pounces. "You."

In between heated kisses, Phil gets the condom on and slathers on lube. Rubbing more lube over my hole, his fingers make a scissor-like motion to prepare me. Once he's prepped my body, and my own cock is standing at attention again, he tangles one hand with mine, using the other to guide himself forward. I lift my hips slightly to make his entry easier.

Then Phil plunges inside, the lube easing his entry and heating me from the inside out. Fuck, I could live forever with him inside of me. The push of his cock filling me, then dragging back against the sensitive tissues as he pulls back, drives me out of my mind. "Phil, baby, harder," I beg.

He just laughs and pushes in again. I can't help the growl in the back of my throat. "Phillip." My voice holds a note of warning. The sounds of our grunting and heavy breathing fill the room. The smell of sex permeates the air as I rake my fingers over his back, knowing I'm marking him and at the same time, driving him over the edge. "Phil, please, now!"

Phil groans his release harshly in my ear, his hands tightening on mine. After his lips release the last sound, I capture his mouth just as my release floods between us both, marking us.

We're immobile, sticky, and not moving for several long minutes before Phil tells me something that eases the burden of yesterday from my soul. "I am so fucking in love with you, Jason. More every day." He lifts his head from my shoulder. "I celebrate being your husband with every beat of my heart."

God, I always know how much I need him. I didn't know how much I needed this.

"I love you, Phillip. I don't know what miracle dropped you into my life..." I'm interrupted by his blinding smile.

"That would be me being a smart-ass to my sisters."

"But I'm so glad our timing was perfect." Running my fingers through his thick blond hair, I tug him down to brush his lips with mine. "You always remind me of that when I need it the most."

Any airs of arrogance drops from his face. It's replaced with haunting residual feelings from a past long fought. Battles he conquered and won. "And you always remind me I'm worth loving, Jason. Never think that either of us gives or takes more than the other when it comes to our love. For us, it's always just enough."

I sigh in pure pleasure, knowing he's right. Telling him, however, would set off a series of catastrophic events that might signal the end of the world as we know it, since he'd lord it over everyone we know.

Phil slides out of me, causing me to wince a little as he's fairly well-endowed. Once he's disposed of the condom and brought back warm washcloths to clean us both up, he crawls back into bed.

Stroking the hair on my chest, he murmurs, "Want to talk about what happened?"

I sigh because I really don't. I know that if I share the burden with Phil, he'll help support me through the holidays as I cycle through the emotions over the loss of a complete stranger. It isn't the first time it's happened since we've been together, and as long as I remain a doctor, it won't be the last.

Holding on to him, I tell him about the events of the day before, as briefly as I can. I feel his hand tighten on mine during the tough parts—moving baby Grace to my vehicle and feeling Mary's life start to fade away. He goes rigid with anger when I tell him about Mary's fiancé.

"How dare he," Phil hisses.

"He needed to vent his anger, babe," I say wearily.

"Not at you. Not at a stranger who went so above and beyond to save everything he loves."

I smile sadly, knowing it doesn't work like that.

Phil pulls me tighter against him and says, "You, my love, deserve a day of pampering."

"It's too bad you have to work," I murmur, wishing we could spend the day together.

"We'll just see about that."

A FEW HOURS LATER, Phil and I are seated in his BMW and heading into New York. I don't know how he managed it, but somehow he talked his sisters into giving him the day off. Even Corinna, who is up to her golden eyes in cake batter, voted yes to throw Phil out for the day.

I know Phil likely shared the details of what happened with my extended family, and it warms my heart to know they fully support me, even if it means they'd all be working late to cover for his share of the burden.

Amaryllis Events, the wedding- and event-planning business my husband founded with his sisters, is one of the premier businesses of its kind in New England and New York. Even though Phil deflects the accolades he deserves for his magic with floral design, it's as much for his artistry as it is for Em's gowns, Corinna's cakes, Holly's photography, and Cassidy and Alison's sharp business and legal eyes that run the firm that draws in as many repeat clients as it does first-time ones. For a man who grew up not only on the edges of poverty, but was weighted down in it with anvils tied around his legs, Phil made a hell of a life for himself and for the five sisters he adopted along the way.

As he turns the wheel, I catch a glimpse of the amaryllis tattoo on the inside of his left wrist—the Freeman family symbol. Each of the siblings has the tattoo in a different location. Phil wanted to be able to see his as he worked with the flowers that feed his soul almost as much as his family and I do.

It hasn't been without tremendous struggle or personal sacrifice that he's made himself into the man who can wear Gucci loafers with ease, but you would never know it from the pride he carries himself with. The pride he taught his sisters to have, who in turn will pass it along to their families when the time is right.

Reaching across the center console, I lay my hand on his thigh. "What are we doing when we get to the city?"

He casts me a quick glance through tinted sunglasses, he muses. "Oh, I thought we'd go visit Keene before I hit up a few stores for his gift. The city has a better selection of porn than Collyer does."

Rolling my eyes, I state clearly, "You are not buying your sister's brother porn for Christmas. It's tacky. It's inappropriate. And..."

"And he probably has enough as it is," Phil concludes sadly. Shaking his head, he laments, "I'm at a loss, then, babe. I just have no idea what to get him."

Grinding my teeth, I offer something bland. Banal. Boring even. "What about a gift card?"

Tapping his finger on the steering wheel, he appears to give it some thought. My spirits soar. This could be momentous—Phil actually listening to a suggestion about Keene without a knock-down, drag-out—

My hopes are dashed when he says, "Nah. I'll think of something. Christmas is still a few days away."

I turn to the door and immediately begin banging my head on the window. I'm almost positive the people in the car next to ours must think I'm a head case. I might be by the time the gift giving is done in three days.

3

"Holy crap, you weren't kidding." I say as we pull into the underground parking beneath Hudson Investigations, the company owned by Keene Marshall and Caleb Lockwood.

It wasn't too long ago we met both of these intriguing men for the first time. Caleb happens to be the older brother of an old friend of mine who I became reacquainted with recently. Ryan, and his now-husband Jared, were looking for a wedding planner to coordinate their wedding in less than two months. Cassidy accepted the job and in doing so, met and fell in love with Caleb, Ryan's older brother.

Little did she know, a large portion of her own personal past would be revealed, and she would uncover the early missing years of her childhood. When all the dust settled, Keene was floored to realize that the woman he'd had interactions with over Ryan's wedding was actually his missing sister of twenty-five years.

Miracles. As a trauma doctor, I hope for them. After falling in love with Phil, I stand as a witness to them.

"Not at all," Phil says cheerfully. He turns his sleek car into a parking spot, putting the car in park. "But only just for a minute. We need to get our parking ticket validated."

I throw my hands up. "Of course we do."

Winking at me, Phil slides out and I make haste to do the same. Meeting at the back of the car, he wraps his arm around my shoulders as we head toward the bank of elevators that will take us directly up to Hudson's executive floor.

"I was having such a good day until you two walked in," I hear behind me. Keene's words would be mildly offensive if he were wearing his trademark smirk. Instead, the compassionate smile gracing his handsome features almost does me in. The normal smirk that typically graces his face is missing and I'm momentarily undone by how much he and Cassidy look alike in that very moment.

Unfortunately, Phil doesn't have that problem. Holding out a hand, Phil comments blandly, "And I wanted to see you so much too, but in the end, I just couldn't decide on what to get you for Christmas, so I brought Jason in to ask his opinion. Do I need to go whole hog and get Ali a vibrator to make up for your shortcomings, or is getting you cock rings in red and green festive enough?"

I suck in air the wrong way, and cough so hard I'm choking. "Phil," I manage to gasp out. A hard whack on my back helps me get my breath back. "Thanks." Turning, I see the wicked cast to Caleb's face. He pulls me away just in time to miss Keene's retort.

"If you tell Phil this, I'll have to kill you, but Keene gets off on their battles," Caleb murmurs to me. He's trying to suppress a huge outburst of laughter as he observes both of his brothers-in-law go at it.

I let out a relieved sigh. "Thank God, because I have no clue what Phil is actually getting him for Christmas. All I've been told is that 'it's going to be epic.' This could mean anything from a subscription to PornHub to Guccis."

Caleb tosses his dark hair back and laughs.

"Hold on a damned second, Keene." Phil literally throws his hand in Keene's face, his own is as excited as a two-year-old. "Baby, did I just hear you say you got me more Guccis for Christmas?"

Keene knocks Phil's hand aside. "You're such a pain in the ass."

He gives Keene a once-over. "Hell no. That would be just tacky to share a man with your own sister."

Keene throws up his hands in exasperation.

Caleb and I are holding each other up we're laughing so hard. Who could have known I needed to laugh so hard? And the realization strikes me. Phil knew. That's who. I don't really understand why we're here, but I fall a little deeper into the infinite spiral of love with Phillip Freeman.

The muted roar of Phil and Keene's battle still wages on. With the understanding that Keene isn't offended, I'm able to enjoy their verbal skirmish: Phil's drawling humor pitted against Keene's dry wit. Something of what I'm feeling must show on my face, because Caleb's voice quietly intrudes into my thoughts. "I couldn't figure out why Phil insisted he had to come up and see us. Now, I get it." Moving in front of me, he claps me on my shoulder. "I never realized until just now how beautifully you balance each other out, Jason." He gives me a quick squeeze and wades off to play referee to two men his wife happens to love.

Most people don't, I think ruefully. They see Phil's prima donna behavior, and not the complex father-like worrier beneath. Those same people presume I'm the level-headed one in our relationship, the doctor who coolly makes life-or-death calls every single damned day. But it's Phil's arms I turn to when I need to find my center, my humanity, and my soul.

Feeling more centered than I have been in the last twenty-four hours, I call out, "Is this the show we came into the city for?" I can't hold back the grin.

"Shit," Keene mutters, a tinge of red crossing his cheekbones. "How is it I let you suck me into an argument when I was planning on being a supportive family member for once?"

Phil goes to open his mouth, and before he can say a word, I step forward and slap my hand across it. Keene's green eyes dance with delight at the move. "I need to learn that trick," he mutters. Shaking his head, he gestures us toward his office. "Come with me for a few,

Jason, and then you can both be on your way. Caleb, you going to join us?"

"Sure. I don't have anything urgent."

As we enter Keene's office with its extraordinary view of the Manhattan skyline, I can't help but notice the portrait of him and Cassidy from when they were children. Phil pauses in front of it, as he does every time he sees it. A smile ghosts around the edge of Keene's lips as he watches my husband's reaction. That's one thing they've never argued over—how much they both love Cassidy, Keene's sister by blood, Phil's by adoption.

"Please, both of you, sit down." Keene gestures to the chairs in front of his desk. "I actually asked Phil to bring you into the office, Jason. It might have surprised you how calm things have been at the house today."

I blink at him. "Now that you said something, I am rather surprised no one's tried to contact me for a comment about what happened yesterday."

Keene's smile is tight. "They've been calling, Jason. Nonstop. Freaking vultures."

"But why haven't I received anything?" I go to reach for my phone to see if it's malfunctioning.

"Because last night when you were on your way home, we had Phil forward all calls to our ops center here at Hudson so we could screen everything. Anything personal, we've been texting Phil about," Caleb interjects gently. "The family and friends of Joseph Bianco are saying he plans on suing for malpractice. Jared's already got one of his friends involved. You're covered under Good Samaritan laws." Jared is Caleb's brother-in-law, now married to his brother Ryan. "The media is going nuts, Jason—inferring you're not on vacation but on suspension. NYU's already issued a statement vehemently denying that fact."

"What you have is a tragic case of someone who lost something precious to them over the holidays, and they're striking back the only way they know how." Keene's voice is grim.

I turn to my husband. "Why couldn't you tell me all of this back at the farm? Why did we come to the city for it?" I'm shocked.

"Because that's not why we came to New York. Caleb and Keene are just offering us a little extra protection from nosy people who aren't invited into our lives," Phil replies.

Flashes of yesterday slam into my brain. All I can see is Mary's blood as I look down at the floor. My ears are ringing with the remembered sounds of Grace's whimpering and her father's bellows. Nausea churns my stomach as I begin to hyperventilate. I lift a shaking hand to my forehead. This is all too much too soon. "Let's just go. I'm sorry for troubling you with all of this. Maybe we should just go home?" I suggest hoarsely, trying to rein in my emotions.

Phil kneels in front of me. "Babe, what is it?"

I dodge him. "It's nothing. Let's just go home. I don't want to be here." I don't want to be anywhere, but knowing my actions have added an additional weight to this already overburdened family is incomprehensible for me in my present state of mind.

Unwillingly, Phil drags me to my feet and pulls me toward the bank of windows. "What do you see?" he asks.

I don't even glance out the expansive bank of windows before I mutter, "The city."

"Really look, and tell me what you see outside of Keene's window. Why would I have parked here at Hudson in all of the places in New York?" Phil grabs me by the shoulders and turns me so I'm flush against the icy panes.

It's impossible to miss when it's so close I can practically touch it. Even from the height we're at, it's an impressive sight—a one hundred foot tall tree with close to 50,000 lights.

The Rockefeller Center Christmas Tree.

"We've gone every year since we started dating. You told me how your parents used to take you as a kid, and we made it our thing." Phil's voice holds determination and strength—a strength I'm desperate to cling to. "Who knows if we were followed here by some reporter or a family member who wants to harass you? I'll never let you be hurt if I can prevent it. I want—no, I need you safe. So, if we have to bring these two with us for our walk around the tree, so be it, but no one gets to take our night from you. From us." Phil crosses his arms over his heart.

A heart I laid my burdens on earlier this morning.

"You won't even know we're there," Keene promises, even as he's shrugging a heavy winter coat on. "Caleb and I will be like any other couple there."

Caleb looks thoughtful. "Okay, but if you don't hold my hand the entire time, I refuse to buy you a hot chocolate."

"Fuck you," Keene says, but without any heat.

"Or that either," is Caleb's quick response.

I let out a bark of a laugh and say, "If you're sure."

Caleb grins at Keene, who rolls his eyes. "Unlike Phil, I don't think it's crass to go on a date with my wife's brother. Let's go."

EVEN FROM BLOCKS AWAY, excitement bubbles around the Rockefeller Center Christmas Tree. Ever since I was a little boy, I've always believed there's a magic about this tree. If I could just get close enough, the wish I would make on its mighty branches would come true.

I wished for the arguing to stop at my house, and while my parents' divorce wasn't ideal to a young child, it certainly was the answer to a prayer.

I wished, as I'm sure many of the young faces looking at the tree with wonder do, for a ton of Christmas presents. I didn't expect to get them, as my Christmas was divided between two homes, but I was blessed by parents who loved me beyond reason even if they'd fallen out of love with each other.

I wished with all my might for an early acceptance letter from Yale my senior year, knowing from an early age I wanted to follow in my father's footsteps and become a doctor. He raced over after I called him, tears in my eyes over my acceptance. It was the first time my father stepped foot back in our old home after cheating on my mother, and she and her new husband answered the door with beaming smiles on their faces.

In that moment, I realized, amidst my euphoria over my acceptance, that life moves on even when it deals you a blow so devastating you're temporarily brought to your knees.

As the bells ring out from people trying to collect money for charities, Phil and I approach the enormous spruce tree. He's been quiet since we left Hudson, leaving me to my thoughts as we navigate our way through the throng of people heading in the same direction we are toward the lights, excitement, and joy. How could you feel anything but those things when you're standing in front of something that's been harvested to represent your Christmas dreams?

"How are you doing?" Phil slips his arm over mine, tugging me close.

I can't look away from the tree just yet. "I'm so glad you brought me. I needed this. I needed to remember…"

"That you're allowed to ask for wishes too?" Phil is astoundingly astute.

"Yes." I lapse back into silence. We stand there for a long time before I close my eyes tightly. Flashes of yesterday run through my mind like the downbeat of a carol.

Love. Frustration. Horror. Fear. Anger. Sadness. Love.

My days always begin and end with love because of the man standing beside me.

Closing my eyes, I make my Christmas wish. Tears leak from beneath my dark lashes and freeze against my cool cheeks.

I only hope someday it will come true.

"Feel better?" Phil whispers, his head tipping to rest against mine.

"Always. I have you." I turn my head to brush my lips gently against his. And it's true. With Phil by my side, I know I'll heal from the loss of a woman I knew for only a few moments, and the words scoring my soul: *"How could you be right there and not manage to save her?"*

Because I can't save them all, no matter how much I wish I could. I'm so sorry I couldn't do it this time.

In the shelter of this magical tree, I try to find the absolution I need to move on and be who I am another day. Dr. Jason Ross.

Pulling back from my kiss with Phillip, I smile.

"Excuse me, sir?" I hear a nasally voice I don't recognize say from behind me. Surprised, I turn and find Keene looking at me as if he doesn't know me. "Would you like us to take a photo for you both? Something for you to remember the tree by?"

I grin at Phil. His devil's smile lets loose. "All right. Do you require a donation before you'll take the picture?" Phil's really getting into his role, remembering that many of the photographers around Rockefeller Center do require a donation for their services.

"Consider this one an early Christmas gift," Keene grumbles. He swings a camera around that looks remarkably like something Holly would use, and takes a few photos. "Do you have a cell phone you'd like for me to use as well?"

"Here." Phil holds his out.

After snapping a few photos, Keene hands the phone back. Stepping closer, so he's not overheard, he murmurs, "Caleb's going to follow you back to the car. I'll see you both at the farm." I shake my head as he seamlessly merges back into the crowd.

"Are you going to tell me what you wished for?" Years ago, I began telling Phil what I had wished for. Keeping my wishes a secret never made any difference on whether or not they came true.

Cupping my husband's cheek, I press a soft kiss to his lips, letting it linger before I answer. "For every member of our family to find a love like ours."

Phil's eyes sparkle in the twinkling light. He swallows as he fights to keep the tears at bay. "Sounds like a perfect wish."

I nod. I thought so too.

4

———

"How did you get your presents wrapped? Did you stay up all night?" I grumble at Phil as I sit at our kitchen table fighting with the scissors, paper, and tape.

Phil shoots me a disdainful look. "Please, let's be real. I paid for the store to wrap them. When I asked Ali to go pick up my gifts, even she wouldn't know the difference between her gift and yours."

I gape at my husband both for his audacity and his genius. Instead of being frustrated with plastic-tape contraptions that claim to cut tape but instead cut your fingers, he's sipping a latte he picked up at The Coffee Shop while watching the weather forecast to determine if we're having a white Christmas.

"You realize there's going to be some pretty insane gift giving this year," I comment absently, trying to make certain the snowmen's heads on my packages line up. Quickly realizing the futility of this effort, I decide time is more important than beauty as I slap another piece of tape on. "I mean, not only is there the regular gift exchange and the white elephant contest, there's now a Secret Santa on top of it." Pausing to admire the way I managed to wrap my entry for the white elephant gift exchange, I sincerely hope that what I bought is considered so grotesque an item that Phil and I only have to host one of these *objets d'horreur* in our home for the following three hundred sixty-four days.

There are a few rules to the annual Freeman white elephant contest. First, the item has to be purchased at HomeGoods. No exceptions. Second, it has to be under fifty dollars, including tax. Third, if you buy the same item as someone else, you're automatically disqualified from winning. Fourth, all family members play—even spouses. I tried to object vehemently to that rule when Phil and I first got married. I was obviously overruled.

But it's the final rule that makes this contest so damn competitive. Whatever object you end up with has to remain on prominent display in your house until the next Christmas Eve when one of the siblings will come around and collect it to be donated after the New Year. Fortunately, Phil pulled off a miracle last year by finding a brownish mustard-yellow magazine bag embroidered with pigs using hot-pink threads. The look on Cassidy's face when she opened it said she knew she was a goner. Until that point, she was in the lead. I wince whenever I pass her entry from last year, a baby-puke-green ceramic lamp in the shape of a guppy resting on our corner table.

With Caleb and Keene now in the running, competition is going to get fierce.

"Babe," I call absently. "Did you wrap your white elephant gift?"

Phil lets out a snort. "I haven't even gone shopping for it yet. You know as well I do, the worst shit is always left for the twenty-third. I thought we'd go today."

I groan, not only knowing he's right but realizing I may have purchased too soon. Eyeing the package I just spent twenty minutes fighting to wrap, I wonder if I should bring it with me in case I need to return it.

Or in case I run into a sibling and they have the same thing in their cart.

～

I DON'T CARE what store you're in, shopping for Christmas on December 23 is a mistake—even if you're looking for the tackiest shit you can find in HomeGoods. Phil and I go up and down every single aisle. My genius husband saw a throw on a display chair as we walked in and snagged it. "Just in case we run into one of the others," he warns.

Good thing he did.

We're down the clearance aisle where the worst and cheapest crap is shoved when we run into Corinna. She's holding a surprisingly normal hot-pink cashmere throw in her hands and admiring it. I pull Phil back behind a display by the back of his jeans. "Shit. I think you just gave me a wedgie," he complains.

"Corinna," I mouth to him, pointing.

Phil's head snaps to attention like a Doberman on the scent of fresh meat. His face screws up in concentration. "That's..."

"Normal," I interject. "It's normal."

"Well, yeah. Jesus, Jason. If that's the worst they have, then your statue of poo is sure to win." Phil slaps a hand over his mouth.

My voice darkens. "How do you know what my entry is, husband dear?"

"Umm..."

"Have you been snooping in the Christmas presents again?" I demand as I push out of our hiding spot.

"Jace, get down. She'll see you," he hisses.

"I don't care." I'm royally pissed.

"I swear I didn't see anything beyond the statue. Once I realized what it was, I closed the door and walked away."

There's one way I can test him. "What did you think of the new Skele-Toes I got you for running? Ali and I talked about them for a long time. She said they'll help a lot with the marathon training she has planned for you this year."

The abject horror on Phil's face can't be faked. He's not that good of an actor. "You've got to be shitting me," he finally whispers.

"Not at all. She says they'll help build up your muscles for endurance. I stopped listening after she said they were the best for you. That's all I want for you to have, baby," I deadpan.

My husband is falling apart in front of me. He's emitting choking sounds that might concern me as a doctor if I didn't know it was from shock.

Behind me, I hear a slow clap. Turning, I'm greeted by Corinna's mischievous grin. "Hey, Cori," I say casually. "Finishing up your white elephant gift shopping?"

"Nah, I bought mine last week. I bribed a stock clerk with a cake to save me some seriously awful crap in the back. I knew I would be too busy to have a chance to shop, and I was not living with another ugly-ass picture frame in my house this year." Corinna's eyes turn feral. "In fact, I may give someone the money for the donation just so I can smash that thing into pieces."

"Is that because of the frame or what's in it?" My husband just has to poke at his sister for receiving a picture of hot military men, thereby reminding her constantly of someone from her past.

Corinna ignores her brother and asks me, "Do you want me to wrap Phil's gift for you and bring it to the family celebration? I guess you had to custom order it since they don't make chastity cages that small?"

Ignoring Phil's sputtering, I answer truthfully, knowing the gift is much more precious than she's insinuating. "If you truly don't mind, it would be appreciated."

She reaches out and squeezes my arm. "Of course not. That's what family does. It will be there Christmas morning."

"I can't believe you hid my gift at Corinna's!" Phil finally yells.

"If I could trust you not to go snooping around like a child for your presents, maybe I wouldn't have to," I answer diplomatically.

Phil storms off in a snit. Corinna and I wait for a half a heartbeat before we both break out into gales of laughter. "Oh, Jason. I was planning to call and give you an update on the kitty, but this was too good to pass up. Quick, take a look in my cart." She drags me over to where her cart has the pink blanket over it. "I found the cutest bed in the pet section that totally complements your bedroom set," she whispers. "The special litter box you ordered came in. It's so beautiful. And trust me, I never thought I'd say that about a place where a cat is going to poo," she snickers. "I picked up the food, bowls, and stand. All I have to do is run to PetSmart to get the litter."

"I am so grateful for everything you did, Cori. He's never going to believe it," I whisper. Phil has wanted a pet for so long but never quite got around to deciding on what he wanted. A few weeks ago, one of my coworkers asked if I wanted to adopt a kitten. When I saw the picture of the kitten sticking its tongue out at me, I knew it was absolutely perfect for Phil. The kitten had attitude wrapped in an adorable package.

Just like my husband.

"Are you two done with your conference yet? I need to finish shopping." Speaking of attitude...

Corinna hastily throws the blanket into her cart. "Did you ever get out of him what he's getting for Keene?"

I answer honestly. "No, I have no clue. I'll find out when the rest of you do."

Phil's slow smile does nothing to ease my fears. "Yes. Yes, you will."

We say our goodbyes before heading in separate directions. Corinna heads to the checkout, leaving Phil and I to comb the store for the worst HomeGoods has to offer.

"I THINK THAT WAS A ROARING SUCCESS," Phil declares as he struggles with the six-foot-high metal parrot that doubles as an umbrella stand.

I look at him doubtfully. I didn't find anything worse than my matte brown glass poo sculpture, so I went with my gut instinct. "How the hell are you planning on wrapping it?" I ask dubiously.

Baby blue eyes look at me through a fringe of lashes imploringly.

"Are you fucking kidding me? Wasn't it bad enough I had to sit with the damn bird's head nestled next to my balls because you didn't want to lower the top?" I roar.

"Someone could have seen him on the way in." Phil's voice has taken on a slightly whiny note. I just know I'm going to end up wrapping the damn bird. Suddenly, an idea takes root.

"You want me to wrap up this piece of shit for you?"

"Yes. I'll do anything."

"Anything?" I repeat. Damnit, now I sound like the damn sculpture.

"Yes, Jace. What do you want?" He trails his fingers up my chest, toying with the buttons on my sweater.

"Genoa. I really want a freaking sandwich from Genoa." I am serious as shit.

"Genoa." Phil's voice goes from seductive to flat in about point two seconds. "I'm offering you anything, and you want..."

"A Cafone. Yes." Sliding my hands around his waist, I nip his ear. "Depending on the kind of mood I'm in after I eat, I might take you up on that other offer."

"If it's still available," he snaps. Stalking away from me, Phil goes through our drop zone and throws his leather coat and gloves back on. Turning back, he gives me a glare. "Anything else?"

"Yeah, one more thing." Stalking toward him, I grab his head with both hands and pull hard. His lips crash onto mine. Moments pass before I release his face and then his lips. "I love you. Drive safely."

Anger dissipating from his eyes, Phil reaches out and gently touches my cheek. "I will. I promise. I'll be back soon."

After he leaves, I cheerfully walk into the garage and grab two paper leaf bags. This bird is going to be wrapped by the time Phil hits the farm gates.

Perfect.

Phil's reaction when he gets back with our food is even better than I anticipated.

"You...bags...people will think that shit is from me! I can't have them think I wrapped that piece of shit like that!" he screeches.

I shrug. My idea of using the paper contractor bags was pretty ingenious. This way, we can use bows, ribbons, and scrap wrapping paper to make it festive. "Be realistic, babe. It doesn't have a box, and anything else I attempted to wrap it with, the damned metal feathers would slice the hell out of."

"Shit." The defeated tone in Phil's voice tells me he didn't think that part through. "Why do I have this feeling we're going to end up with a parrot because no one will pick it?"

"You think?" I say sarcastically. "And better yet, a parrot who's already tried to suck down my balls."

Phil begins to laugh. "Maybe we should keep him then. Frisky little bugger."

"Let's not and say we did."

Tossing an arm over my shoulder, my husband guides me to the island separating our kitchen from where I've been wrapping gifts. "Just think, babe. I guess that makes you more of an ornithologist than me."

"That's the study of birds, Phil. Not when the birds study you."

"Hmm, true. Maybe a Poe-ologist then?"

"Falling into madness over love? That sounds about right." We both grin even as we sit down to have lunch.

Somehow, I know he's right, and that damn bird will end up coming back with us, but that's okay. It will be a complete menagerie around here between Phil, the bird, and the new kitten he knows nothing about.

5

A night where we hope the whole world experiences peace.
No matter your race, wealth, religion, sexual orientation, political beliefs, or lack of any, may you find peace this one night surrounded by people who love you down to the core of your soul. May love's pure light keep you glowing warm from the inside out so the holes in your heart seem to mend.

That's what Christmas Eve means to me.

I'm standing in the nondenominational church in Collyer where many of the residents have come to listen to not only the service but the a cappella choir. The cafetorium is so crowded, the reverend decided to limit seating to just the few who absolutely needed to sit to ensure all who showed would fit. Everyone else was asked to stand.

Even with Phil's arm supporting me, I shift from one foot to the other. I feel anxious, and I can't understand why.

As Pastor McGowan finishes his sermon about how the birth of Christ is a celebration, I feel a hard jostle in my side that knocks me into Phil, throwing us both off balance. Righting myself, I meet the hate-filled eyes of Joseph Bianco.

"No amount of absolution will save you, Doc. Not if I have

anything to say about it," he hisses. He's clutching a squirming bundle close to his chest. Baby Grace.

Heartbroken, I feel Phil push up close behind me. People around us start to murmur. "Let's step outside, Mr. Bianco," I suggest quietly. "Leave these people to their peace."

"Why the hell should they get peace when I don't have any?" The room around us gets abnormally quiet. Even Pastor McGowan gets quiet at the pulpit. "How long did you stand there before you did anything, Doctor?" he sneers. "How long did my fiancée lie there dying before you got your precious hands dirty?"

"Long enough for me to move your child to safety." His shocked gasp doesn't come as a surprise. Joseph pulls back far enough to look down into baby Grace's face and pales. "I moved her to my vehicle and immediately began triaging the situation. Mary told me she was only two months old. I wanted to make sure she was safe," I choke out. I can't stop the tears that fall anymore. "I'm so sorry. I did everything I could. I'm just a man." My head drops and I lift my hands slightly. "I'm just a man."

Joseph opens his mouth to speak and then closes it, pulling Grace tight to him.

Phil tugs me gently. "Come on, Jace. We're leaving." I nod, too emotionally raw to stay.

A voice intrudes. "No, Dr. Ross, Mr. Freeman. It's Joseph who will be leaving." A burly man who I know I've run into occasionally at The Coffee Shop, clasps Joseph by the shoulders. "Come on, son. Let's go home. "

Eyes glistening, a broken Joseph Bianco looks up at his father before nodding.

The senior Bianco pushes his son in front of him gently, before turning back to me. "Thank you, Dr. Ross. It's hard to imagine now, but what you just told him will eventually penetrate to help him start to heal." Nodding, he disappears into the crowd that seems to hug me and Phil as they close back around us.

Slowly, too slowly, the buzz in the room picks up. Without another word, Pastor McGowan gestures to the choir. Within seconds,

I'm sobbing against my husband, letting out all of my frustration, anger, and hopelessness at not being able to save a young woman for her family as the strains of "Silent Night" surround us.

WITH MY MOTHER on a cruise with her husband, and my father on call for the holiday, this is the first Christmas Eve in a long time where Phil and I don't have plans to drive to one of their houses immediately after mass to spend the rest of the evening with one of my parents. While I was disconcerted by that earlier in the month, after the confrontation at the church, I'm incredibly grateful.

I want nothing more than to be home wearing an old sweatshirt, flannel pajama pants, and sitting in front of a fire with an eggnog heavy on the bourbon. I thought with all of the extra love and care I've been receiving from Phil this week, I'd begin to recover from the events that happened just a few short days ago.

I was wrong.

I am no more healed from the loss of the woman who wasn't even technically my patient than any of the others I've lost on the table in my ten years of medicine.

My head leans against the cold window as Phil navigates his way deftly through the streets. I'm so out of it, I don't realize he's pulled up to a cemetery until we've actually stopped. "What are we doing here?" I'm baffled.

"I'm trying to give you some closure," Phil says quietly. "Come on."

Sliding out of the warm car, I burrow deeper into my coat. Love is equal parts companionship, lust, faith, and trust. I trust that whatever Phil is about to do won't harm me further than anything else has tonight, but maybe it will close some of the fissures in my cracked heart.

Phil pulls something from the back seat of the car. It's a bouquet of white roses and forget-me-nots. New tears fall from my cheeks, different from the helpless ones I shed at services. The ones falling now are because my husband knows on this night, I need to find something that's been eluding me.

Peace.

"Come on, babe. She's over here." Phil's voice is low. He takes my hand and guides me up the withered stone stairs. Our feet crunch on the frozen grass surrounding each plot as we make our way to the recently upturned ground.

There's no marker; it's too soon for that. I imagine her family chose something beautiful for the new mother especially if the riotous blooms that are slowly decaying in the December cold are anything to go by. It's too soon. They should last longer.

Much like Mary's life.

"Her last name was Moss. Mary Moss," Phil tells me. "I read the obituary online."

I nod, unable to speak.

"Do you want me to tell you more?"

"Yes."

"She was a schoolteacher. He's a fireman. They were planning a summer wedding."

"Were you..." The rest of my question is unasked, but unnecessary.

"No, they weren't using us to run their wedding, but we've already made calls to all of their vendors. Every single one is returning their deposits. One refused, but we handled it."

"Of course you did," I exhale.

"Of all things, it was for the stupid cake. Like they were out any money. Corinna had a fit." Phil's change of tone tells me he's about to let loose one of his famous rampages.

"Calm yourself, honey," I whisper gently.

Phil inhales a deep breath. "Right. As I was saying, they were a sweet love that ended up with a beautiful baby." Phil looks down at the gravesite sadly. "He'll always have that living piece of her."

"Yeah, he will." I send up a silent prayer that nothing ever happens to that precious baby girl.

Phil kisses my cheek before sliding the bouquet into my hand. "I'll be by the car. Take all the time you need."

I stand there as Phil moves away to wait for me to do something I've never done before.

Say goodbye to a patient I've lost at their final resting place.

I clear my throat. "Hi, Mary. I'm Jason. We didn't really know each other for more than a few moments. I think we'd both like a do-over." My head drops. God, was there something I could have done differently? Could I have saved this young mother?

"You deserved to see your little girl grow up, Mary," I barely manage to choke out. "You deserved to see her crawl, walk, and talk. You deserved to see her dance in the flowers and dance at her wedding. You deserved to see her open presents at Christmas." I swipe at the tears flowing from my eyes. "I'm so sorry I couldn't do more for both of you—for all of you," I amend, thinking of the pain in Joseph Bianco's eyes. "All I can do is wish you peace." Bending down, I lay the fresh bouquet I know my husband spent hours on because of its importance to me. Straightening, I feel a whisper of cold wash through me, taking away my feelings of guilt.

While my remorse will never go away, I can't continue to feel guilty for something I didn't do. I wasn't the person who hit Mary Moss at such a speed. I didn't take her life. I offered all I could do to help save her for this life.

It was out of my hands and now in God's.

Clouds shift and the path back toward my husband is bathed in golden moonlight. I walk along that golden path to the warm arms waiting for me.

I'm ready to go home to finish my healing there.

6

"Merry Christmas!" is shouted at me from all directions as Phil and I enter the barn for the first time. I grin from ear-to-ear. How could I not when the first person I see is dressed in an elf hat, striped tights, and cutoff jean shorts? Not to mention, red, white, and green tie-dyed Chucks?

And that's just what Corinna has on.

The Freemans are notorious for being a little crazy when they're all together. Add in the spirit of the holiday season, and the great room of the barn looks like a Christmas superstore vomited all over the place. Garland and lights are strung from the high beams, bouncing sparkling light everywhere. The massive Christmas tree we decorated right after Thanksgiving stands tall and proud near the windows overlooking the lake. The smells of coffee, hot chocolate, and hot cider permeate the air as well as Corinna's decadent cinnamon rolls, making my mouth water. And that's only the first of the delicious things we'll be eating throughout the day.

I lower my armful of bags and wrapped packages to the floor just as a body crashes into me. Holly gives me a massive hug. "Merry Christmas, Jace. I can't wait to give you your gift."

I laugh. Even though the Secret Santa draws were supposed to be secret, everyone knows who everyone else has. I drew Em, which was actually a challenge. I wanted to get her something meaningful, so I enlisted Cassidy's help. I think she's going to love it. "You can torture me about my gift in a few more minutes," I joke. "Let me go get more presents out of the car."

"There's no need," I hear from behind me. I see Keene and Caleb struggling with the package containing Phil's white elephant entry while my husband strolls in with his perfectly decorated shopping bags. "You take it easy, Jason. We'll help Phil unload," Keene announces rushing out the door.

I have to admit I'm surprised—until Ali snorts out a laugh on my other side. "He was fine until we all started belting The Waitresses and shaking it, Jace. Then I think he started to panic because I knew every word." Ali rubs her hand over her barely noticeable baby bump. "Since we found out she's a girl, he keeps looking at our antics like I can pass them down through the placenta. If you could take him aside and reassure him of that, I'd appreciate that more than anything you might have bought me." She leans over to brush her lips against my cheek, then skips off to help Corinna in the kitchen.

Cassidy moves in next, holding a twin in each arm. "Here, take one." Plopping a baby in my arms, I look down to see I have little Laura. Instinctively, I begin to sway with her to the melody of the music. "These babies are going to be so spoiled. No one ever puts them down," Cassidy sighs.

"Better too much love than not enough," I remind her.

Her face brightens. "True enough." Her dark hair is braided and tucked under a Santa hat. Laura's twin, Jonathan, is fascinated with the pompom bounces back and forth against her dark hair. "There can never be enough love."

"Speaking of that..." I frown. Obviously, Laura doesn't like the look on my face as she flails a little hand and smacks me on the lips. I grin down at the precious bundle in my arms, who has not a clue what she's doing. It's not long before we hear Corinna call out, "Breakfast is up! Come get it while it lasts!"

Caleb comes over just as I'm making my way to the long farm-style table. "Hand her over, Jason. I'm used to eating one-handed," he says ruefully.

I shake my head. "Go ahead and eat, Caleb. As long as I get one of those cinnamon rolls and coffee, I'm good." Corinna, hearing me, begins to load my plate for me.

"There's nothing you can't just eat with a fork, Jason. You sure you don't want anything else?"

I shake my head. "I'm saving room for later."

Everyone groans. Food isn't something in short supply on Christmas Day. We'll have trays of cold cuts and cheese, and every kind of chips and dip imaginable. For dinner, Corinna goes all out with a roast prime rib, Yorkshire pudding, cornbread casserole, stuffing with bacon, and an assortment of other side vegetables. Not to mention her infamous desserts, now made more famous since she recently appeared on an episode of *Caketastic* on Food Network.

We don't waste time lingering over breakfast before we refill our drinks of choice and head over to the presents. Phil and Cassidy exchange glances.

Oh, God. Here it comes. The Freeman White Elephant Exchange. I begin to brace.

"Do we need to go over the rules again?" Phil drawls over the hooting and hollering of his siblings. Caleb and Keene groan as loud as I do.

"I don't know about going over the rules, but I think we put whatever the hell that thing is"—Cassidy flicks her finger in a wonky circle at Phil's parrot entry—"in a stationary spot. Whoever gets stuck—I mean, blessed, with it, should move to it."

"Since it took two of us to move it without ruining the wrapping, I vote yes," Caleb concurs. Keene nods his assent, eyeing the package as if it might strike.

Since I know for a fact it attacks the male anatomy when it gets too close, Keene's wariness is not unwarranted.

Phil claps his hands together. "All right then, someone give me a hat." Em whips off the red and green striped hat she's wearing. "This

is to make certain my darling sister doesn't accuse me of cheating."
Phil eyes Cassidy.

"Listen, there was no damn way you didn't cheat by pulling your
own name the last three years in a row."

Phil looks affronted when his siblings snicker. "To be fair," Phil
sneers, making me want to jump him and kiss the pout off his lips,
"everyone will place their own folded card in the hat, and someone
else will place my name in. Every round someone else will choose the
next victim—I mean recipient."

Everyone laughs.

He claps. "Okay! Are we ready? Let the games begin!" Phil yells.
The hooting and hollering pick up to an epic level. All I can think is
it's a good thing babies sleep well, as I look at the warm bundle of
sweetness still in my arms.

And boy do they begin.

This year, people are even more vicious in stealing perceived "better" gifts, even from their spouses and significant others. And no one
wants Phil's parrot. It's like watching musical chairs as people shift in
and out of the chair next to that beast of a package as quickly as
possible. I'm humored to see Cassidy clutch her bundle to her like it's
the Holy Grail.

Suddenly, inspiration strikes. I eye Phil's monstrosity again.
Leaning over to Corinna, I whisper a few words in her ear. She looks
at me and says, "That's superb."

Phil's eyes narrow. I can practically see the wheels turning. He has
no idea what's about to happen.

I just hope it works out.

Finally, it's just Corinna, Phil, and me left. Caleb calls out,
"Corinna."

She winks at me. Standing with her gift in her hand, she walks
around the room, playing a wicked game of Duck, Duck, Goose with
her family. Finally stopping in front of Ali, her brilliant smile comes
out. "Hand it over, sister."

"Damn," Ali mutters. "I thought I was safe."

Corinna cackles. "It's never safe until it's over."

Ali curses her sister under her breath and reluctantly exchanges gifts.

Corinna sits back down and accepts the hat from Caleb. She reaches in and calls out, "Phil."

Phil's grin can only be classified as evil. He doesn't hesitate. He stalks over to Cassidy and snatches the gift from her like a cantankerous two-year-old. "No," she whimpers.

"Take the chair." Phil's voice is diabolical, setting the family off in hysterics.

I'd feel bad for Cassidy if I wasn't about to save her.

Phil turns to me and pulls my name, the last name, out of the hat. "Sweetheart," he coos, even as he tosses the hat back in Em's face. She sputters and curses him, almost dropping her white elephant gift.

To make this look good, I stand, holding my gift and the baby. I circle the room, slowly. I pause to admire Corinna's gift and get a subtle wink. I meet Keene's glare head-on, and I grin when he growls. This is too much fun. Then I reach a defeated Cassidy, who's eyeing the monstrosity with despair.

"Cass? Honey?" I hold out the poo statue, which I know will be less painful for her than the parrot. She fumbles it around before she clasps it.

She looks confused, then wondrous. "Are you serious?" she whispers.

I chuckle out loud, even as Phil is yelling, "What the hell are you doing, Jace?"

"Corinna?" I call out. "It's time." She scurries upstairs to get Phil's Christmas gift. "Cass, here, take Laura, and then you need to move." After taking her daughter, she quickly vacates her chair. I sit. "Phil, can you come unwrap my gift for me?"

"You're crazy, Jason." But he does as I ask. Everyone bursts out laughing when the head of the yellow and green metal parrot becomes exposed. The narrow base, which is intended for umbrellas, appears.

"Jason, whatever you need for the next decade, it's yours," Cassidy declares fervently.

Suddenly, amid the noise and laughter, you can hear it.

Mew.

I pull Phil onto my lap. "If we wrap the bottom with twine and weight it down, won't it make a great scratching post when he's older, babe?"

Phil's not breathing. His jaw is unhinged as Corinna carries the tiny little kitten toward him. "Merry Christmas, brother, from your amazing husband." Corinna kisses him on the cheek as she hands him my gift.

Phil holds the kitten in his hand, all machinations from the white elephant erased from his face. "You got me a kitty?" His face is radiant.

"You said you wanted one." This reaction is almost better than I expected.

"I never...He's so...I love you so much." Phil tucks his head in my neck and sobs.

Phil told me something I've never forgotten, something he's never shared with his sisters. Before meeting Cassidy, a ratty old cat was what kept him company in between his "father's" beatings. Being able to stroke that flea-riddled cat was what kept him sane.

"How about we open the rest of the white elephant gifts later?" Cassidy suggests. Moving from where she was perched on Caleb's knees, she walks over to us. "You're a good man, Jason Ross." She brushes her lips against the top of my head, then moves away.

I nuzzle the top of my husband's head. "What are you going to name him?"

"I don't know." Phil's voice is filled with wonder.

Immediately, the family starts chiming in with cute names like Tiger, Fluffy, and Batter, when suddenly, Keene comes out with the perfect name. "Rebel. After all, look who his dad's going to be?"

"Rebel," Phil murmurs, stroking his small head. *Mew.* "It's perfect, Keene." Phil flashes him a winning smile. "And since we're going out of order, I've waited for too long to give you this."

Phil hands me Rebel and says, "Watch out for our baby." Sliding off my lap, he goes to the pile of gifts on the floor. Reaching for the largest of the bags, he picks it up and walks it over to Keene. "Here's your Secret Santa gift. Merry Christmas, Keene."

Everyone eyes the package suspiciously, especially Keene. "Thank you, Phil."

A smile hovers around my husband's lips. "I really think you'll like it. There are a few parts." Phil returns to my lap and takes Rebel back, stroking his head immediately.

Keene looks at the gift warily before he pulls out the tissue. Three gifts are wrapped inside: one small and two large. He looks at Phil. "Which should I start with?"

"The small one."

Keene carefully undoes the wrapping, and inside is a book. I sincerely hope it's not a copy of the *Kama Sutra*. It's not.

It's L. Frank Baum's, *A Kidnapped Santa Claus*.

"Read what I wrote," Phil says softly. Keene flips the book to the title page and reads aloud.

Keene,

I'm not comparing you to Santa. There's not a chance in hell of that. I just thought you might appreciate the fact that Santa needed to rely on someone else to do his most important duty for a while—his elves. They all wanted the same thing. A perfect Christmas for those they love.

We're glad to have another brother in our family.

Phillip

Keene's hands are shaking as he closes the book. "Thank you, Phil. This means so much even without the other gifts."

Phil's smile broadens. "Open the red one first."

Without another word, Keene carefully opens the glossy red paper. Inside is a matte black box, which Keene slowly lifts the lid off of. Wordlessly, he lifts out a thick photo album to an almost silent room except for the occasional squeak from the kitten. Turning the cover, he makes a choked sound. "Sweet Jesus, Phil." Ali, who's sitting next to him, wraps her arm around him and leans into him close.

"What is it?" Emily calls from her seat on the far side of the room.

Keene obviously can't speak. He's too busy wiping tears from his eyes. Ali manages to choke out, "It's an album of pictures of Cass as a little girl."

"Since the time we met," Phil confirms.

"Oh, Phil," Cassidy breathes.

"I had a lot of help," Phil admits. He nods toward Holly. "If I wasn't going through photos, she was. Not just for this album either." Keene's head snaps up.

"There's more?" Keene's smile is enormous.

Phil nods. "Open the green box."

This time, Keene tears into it with excitement. Tossing the lid on the floor, he opens the flap of the second album while it's still in the box. He whoops with laughter while Ali groans. "Jesus, Phil. All of my photos too?"

The room breaks into laughter.

"I don't suppose I escaped the pictures of my hair dyed red in this?" Corinna is laughing at Ali, while Holly shakes her head. A retribution prank Corinna pulled on Ali was masterfully captured by Holly on camera while they were in college.

"Oh, those are in there. Believe you me," Phil drawls.

Putting the albums down, Keene stands and approaches us. "Phil?" He extends his hand.

Phil carefully hands me his kitten. Extending his own hand, he's surprised when Keene pulls him into a back-slapping hug. "Thank you. From the bottom of my heart, thank you for watching over them, and thank you for this gift." Keene's voice is rough.

"Both were absolutely my pleasure."

7

Not long after, we begin opening the rest of the white elephant gifts. Unsurprisingly, Cassidy is ridiculously thrilled with her brown glass statue that looks like poo versus the parrot she could have been stuck with. Even Caleb is happy with the brass bull that is about two feet long. Looking down at his son, he said it would make a good doorstop for his room.

Ali and Keene look at each other and burst out laughing when they open the exact same gift—a foot-tall golden plastic statue of a head that resembles the Egyptian god Isis. Even knowing this takes them out of the running for eliminating one of their gifts for ugliest gifts, Ali looks at Keene with practicality. "We have two homes. We can stick one in each."

Corinna has a wreath of seashells, which she says isn't so bad. "I can hang spices from it if nothing else." She shrugs.

Phil unwraps a vase that incidentally matches the bright yellow feathers on our bird. It's an atrocious color, but other than that, there's really nothing wrong with it. He looks at me and curses. "Damn."

It's really down to Em and Holly.

Em unwrapped a statue that Holly found, which looks like a

twisted, coiled snake with no face. It's creepy, freaky, and ugly as all hell. Holly has a deranged brass guppy that's smiling like Bruce the Shark from *Finding Nemo*. From a fear-factor perspective, I'm probably going to vote for Em because I'd be afraid of finding that snake's face in the middle of the night.

Apparently, so was everyone else.

Em dances around the room like she just won an Olympic gold medal or an Academy Award. "Who-hoo! I'm free. Three hundred and sixty-four days of decorative freedom!"

Soon the room is a chaotic eruption of paper. Phil's the only one being careful as he's holding Rebel close to his heart. I smile as Em tears up over the cameo of her Aunt Dee's face. The way her fingers trace over the cameo's delicate surface is thanks enough, even before she launches herself out of the chair at me.

Cassidy blanches, then hurls herself into Keene's arms over a perfectly matched set of pearls that were her mother's. Caleb fastens complementary drop pearl earrings in her ears, causing her to weep. Caleb's gift was a series of photographs of Cassidy and the babies that Holly had taken, along with a promise they'd be updated every three months over the first year. Since Caleb spends a good amount of time working, he always worries he's not around enough with his wife and twins.

Ali's gifts are also extraordinary. Diamonds have been their thing since Keene placed the pendant that was his mother's around her neck. For Christmas, he slides a diamond bangle on her delicate wrist, kissing the underside and murmuring something none of us can hear. She returns the gift by giving him a pair of engraved cufflinks with a diamond chip in them. Even with all the bling, Ali still sparkles more than the diamonds due to the life growing inside of her.

Em is astounded when she realizes her siblings chipped in and are sending her to Paris on an open-ended ticket so she can worship at the altar of her fashion idols. Holly admires her new leather camera bags that were custom made, and are so soft, none of us are surprised when Rebel crawls inside for a nap.

But it's Corinna's gift to us all that steals the show. She hands out manila envelopes to all of us, asking us all to wait before opening them. Once she sits down, she waves her hand and says, "Okay, go ahead," but she's watching us closely.

We all pull out a black-and-white headshot of Brendan Blake, country musician megastar. They're all signed *Look forward to meeting you! ~BB.*

"What does this mean, Cori?" Holly asks.

"Well," Corinna drawls, "since Brendan and I remained friends after *Caketastic*"—the Food Network show she kicked ass on—"he asked if I'd be interested in seeing him play. Block off your calendars in June, because we've all got backstage tickets to Brendan Blake!"

The noise level in the barn just broke the sound barrier as the Freemans start jumping around and screaming. Rebel hisses from his spot inside Corinna's camera bag. "Oh, God. If they're this bad now, can you imagine the night of the concert?" Keene moans. But his eyes are sparkling.

Caleb agrees. "It's going to be epic."

I nod. "It's going to be something."

Corinna laughs amid the noise. "I got tickets for Ryan, Jared, and Charlie too. I mean, the whole family is coming." This, of course, sets the whole family off again, only now they're singing one of Brendan Blake's country ballads en masse.

Caleb lifts up his phone and starts recording it. "Never know when you might need it," he murmurs as an aside to me and Keene.

Before long, we're being pulled into the circle of happiness by this family forged of love, of pride, and of strength. Hugs and kisses are exchanged all around. When I reach my husband, I pull his head toward me and cover his mouth with mine for a long kiss I hope conveys everything I feel about him. Not only at this moment, but for every moment since we met.

Honor. Love. Loyalty. Passion. Faith. Trust. Pride.

And those are only a few of the things I can think of while my head is buzzing from the return kiss Phil gives me back. Rubbing his nose against mine as we break apart, he whispers, "Thank you for making every day a celebration, Jace."

And that's it. With Phil, every day is a celebration of our love, our life, and our family.

All in all, this has been a pretty spectacular Christmas already, and we haven't even got to the feast Corinna has cooked. I've been blessed by so much. Yet, while I've been blessed by gifts, I only hope my wishes come true.

8

SIX MONTHS LATER

"**D**r. Ross! Hey, Dr. Ross! Can you wait up?" a voice I don't recognize calls behind us, as Phil and I exit the Danbury Fair Mall.

I haven't been back much since Christmas, but Phil wanted to go before we head to the Brendan Blake concert tonight. I laughed at the bra he bought to toss on stage. It's an obnoxious orange color with neon green stripes. If it weren't only four dollars, I'd have vehemently fought him on buying it.

Both Phil and I turn. I'm frozen in place when Joseph Bianco walks up to us at a fast clip, pushing a stroller. He looks tired but much less haggard than when we saw him on Christmas Eve. Not even winded when he reaches us, he smiles when he stops. "Thank you both for waiting."

"It's not a problem, Mr. Bianco," I say quietly. I feel Phil's arm slip around my waist in support.

"Please, Dr. Ross. Call me Joe." He tentatively holds out his hand.

I blink a few times, but I take his hand. He squeezes it appreciatively. "I appreciate your time. I've wanted to contact you for a long time, but the hospital said you weren't staffed there."

He's wanted to contact me? I'm about to ask why when he beats me to it. "I owe you a huge apology, Dr. Ross. I was in a horrible place when I lost Mary. I didn't know—and I still don't if I am being truthful—what to do with a baby girl. I lashed out at everyone. Mary's family, my family, the hospital, you. But no one more than you." He swallows hard before reaching into the stroller for his squirming baby.

Grace. "She's gotten so big," I muse aloud.

Smiling down at the baby girl who is pointing at me from his arms, he asks, "Would you like to hold her?"

"I'd love to," I say honestly. Stepping away from Phil, I reach for the little girl, who still has those perfect bow lips. Grace practically dive bombs from her father's arms into mine. This is obviously a very loved child.

"Hey, baby girl." I snuggle her in my arms expertly since I've had plenty of practice between Cassidy's Laura and Jonathan and Ali's Kalie. I look down at her mouth blowing raspberries. "Has she been teething?" I ask Grace's father.

Joe laughs. "Oh yeah. I freaked out when she spiked the fever that comes along with it. I panicked on the phone so hard with my mother, and all she did was laugh. I've had a few fun nights since where she's sucked frozen washcloths dry, but the best was when she gnawed on the end table."

I grin at the new father. "I'm glad you have such a good support system."

"Yeah, I do." His face takes on a cast of sadness. "It's not the kind of support I was hoping for, but they've been fantastic."

I smile sadly.

"Anyway, I just wanted the opportunity to say thank you. I know you did everything you could—more than could be expected." Grace starts to get fussy. I pass her back over to her father, who reaches into the stroller for a Binky. "But it was knowing how you saved part of my heart that really began turning the tide."

We all go silent, remembering our confrontation on Christmas Eve.

"We have to get going," Phil interjects. "We have to be back at the office soon."

"I didn't realize I was keeping you," Joe quickly apologizes.

I wave at both Joe and my husband. "That's not a problem." Reaching into my pocket, I pull out my business card. "If you ever need anything—looking for a good pediatrician, or whatever else— don't hesitate to call."

Joe looks down at the card, then back up at me. "Thank you, Dr. Ross."

I hold out my hand. "Jason," I tell him firmly. "And this is my husband, Phil."

Joe shakes my hand again, before reaching for Phil's. "Again, I appreciate everything."

"That's just who I am." I shrug. We say our goodbyes, and Phil and I start to make our way to the exit.

"Jason! One last thing!" Joseph calls out. I wait as he straightens from where he had just placed Grace back in her stroller. "Would you know anything about the bouquets of white roses and forget-me-nots being delivered to Mary's grave each month?"

I turn to Phil in surprise. My husband just shrugs. I reply, "I think I have an idea of who it is."

"Be sure to thank them for me. It's awfully generous."

Joe tosses up his hand and walks away. As he does, I lean forward and touch my lips to Phil's. There is nothing quite like love. The man standing next to me proves that every day. I just hope the man who walked away can find it again someday so he can experience what I've found.

A love to rejoice in.

ALSO BY TRACEY JERALD

Midas Series

Perfect Proposal

Perfect Assumption (Coming April 2021)

Perfect Composition (Coming Summer 2021)

Perfect Order (Coming Fall 2021)

Amaryllis Series

Free - An Amaryllis Prequel

(Newsletter Subscribers only)

Free to Dream

Free to Run

Free to Rejoice

Free to Breathe

Free to Believe

Free to Live

Free to Wish: An Amaryllis Series Short Story - 1,001 Dark Nights Short Story Anthology Winner

Free to Dance (Coming Spring 2021)

Glacier Adventure Series

Return by Air

Return by Land

Return by Sea

Sandalones

CLOSE MATCH

RIPPLE EFFECT

Lady Boss Press Releases

CHALLENGED BY YOU

ACKNOWLEDGMENTS

To my husband and son, who both understood I was absolutely insane when I decided to write a novella in between two huge books. Thank you for loving me despite my being a lunatic.

To my mother, for giving me beautiful Christmases to remember. I love you!

Jen, for being the Christmas spirit in my life every day.

To my Meows; I lived with that gold head on my mantel for YEARS. There's a reason I no longer have a fireplace, and it's not because I live in Florida. I love you all!

Jennifer Wolfel, thank you for everything you do, big and small. You have my eternal gratitude.

To Sandra Depukat from One Love Editing. You saved Christmas! Love you!

To Trifecta Editing Services. Thank you for adding this in! You all are definitely on Santa's nice list.

My cover and brand designer, Amy Queue of QDesigns, You hit this snowball out of the park!

To the team at Foreward PR. Linda Russell – You are the best gift I asked for on Santa's wish list. To Alissa Marino - I was blessed Santa thought I was a good long enough to bring you in my life too!

To all of the bloggers who are reading this, thank you. Every time you read my work, I am truly honored.

To my readers, this story is for you. I hope you loved seeing a deeper insight into Jason and Phil. Happy holidays!

ABOUT THE AUTHOR

Tracey Jerald knew she was meant to be a writer when she would re-write the ending of books in her head when she was a young girl growing up in southern Connecticut. It wasn't long before she was typing alternate endings and extended epilogues "just for fun".

After college in Florida, where she obtained a degree in Criminal Justice, Tracey traded the world of law and order for IT. Her work for a world-wide internet startup transferred her to Northern Virginia where she met her husband in what many call their own happily ever after. They have one son.

When she's not busy with her family or writing, Tracey can be found in her home in north Florida drinking coffee, reading, training for a runDisney event, or feeding her addiction to HGTV.

To follow Tracey, go to her website at http://www.traceyjerald.com. While you're there, be sure to sign up for her newsletter for up to date release information!

Made in the USA
Columbia, SC
07 July 2021